A. N. Irvano was born in 1990 in California and still lives in the area. This is the author's fourth book and first collection of short stories.

Falling Horse Books

Falling Horse Books

With Kindness

Copyright © 2014 A.N.Irvano

First Edition

Book Design: A.N. Irvano

ISBN: 978-0-9960346-4-7

Library of Congress

Printed in the United States of America

WHAT
WE
CAN
NOT
DO

Anthology of Stories by
A. N. Irvano

Table of Contents

"The interpretation of our reality
through patterns not our own, serves only to make
us ever more unknown, ever less free, ever more
solitary."
Gabriel Garcia Mundez

TALK OF THE GROUND

Insidious as they became, they started very quietly. Saying things that only the most quiet people would ever hear. For weeks at a time, they were largely regarded as trifles of the listeners' ears. Above suspicion, the real threat went largely unnoticed.

Like a victim of some horrific, nearly debilitating accident, the menace grew in strength over a slow amount of time. Once nominal, they became historic. The first few targets did not even truly know what it was they were dealing with. Most of the suicides were attempted because the people believed they themselves had gone unhinged. Thinking they were mad with delusions, it seemed almost compulsory.

Whispers of sounds and consonants began their development. They were not goo's and ga's as if they were humans babies, but true tries at words and phonemes. Those voicing had studied. Not just in their lifetime had they studied, but generation and generation before had known the sounds and words like a child knows their blankets. They had an inherent knowledge, but the skill came slowly.

In the first week, a woman shot herself in the head, a second woman took her son's oxyconton that she had secretly known about for months and died, and another three men hung themselves from pipes and beams that collapsed, since either the rope was evidence and taken away or the weight of the body caused breakage.

For two weeks, the hydrangea bush outside of Jeff's building said his last name to him as he got into his car. He had a driver, as was fit for Jeff. He believed the voice, an overtaxed peal falling on his ears, to be his driver speaking to him. The gentlemen's odd habit was inconsistent, for Jeff heard him only say his name when they were beginning their drives in the morning or during a time of the day when they stopped in at his apartment.

He put his finger against the ombré upholstery inside of the door. He watched himself tap out his index finger, then began looking to his driver and inhaling. He was going to tell him that he had realized that he only called his name outside of the brownstone, but recognized that it was such a trite, insignificant, minuscule, and ultimately irreproachable behavior that inducing discussion based on it would be too, too much. He liked the relationship he had with his driver, he didn't want to start anything too insincere.

"Goldblum," came the declaration one morning and Jeff stopped, looking candidly at his driver. His driver looked back at him, not one to remain stoic for long, he smiled and waved an arm towards the backseat, his other arm holding the door open.

"No," Jeff said, raising a finger and leaving his mouth open.

"Is everything all right, sir?" his driver asked, concern dripping from his eyes.

Jeff saved face and nodded reassuringly, smiling, nodding, even. "Quite all right, Franklin, it is. I just could have sworn you were speaking to me, even though you were not talking." His driver breathed in deeply, looking away from Jeff as if something concerned him. "It's really nothing," Jeff said as he tucked his coat up to get in the backset.

"No, sir," Franklin interjected as he put an arm out to stop Jeff from getting in. "I think I have an idea about what you're talking about, problem is, nobody but us it out here, are they?"

"So you heard it, too?" Jeff asked, ducking into the car. He was committed to retaining his self-respect and bundled his coat over his knees. "Let's move, shall we?"

Franklin looked up and down the street and moved his jaw closer to his chin, nodding and saying to himself, "Let's."

"Franklin," came a tiny, nubile voice, before it giggled and repeated Jeff's last name over and over until the sun went down.

Jeff had stayed away for the day and stayed away that night, too. He worried that day, about just as much as he had worried about the filtering of lovely people from his life or where he would go tomorrow. He had his driver take him to stare at the ocean. They both sat against the hood of the car and desolately ate sandwiches as they watched the impending waves that crashed towards them but never quite reached them.

Jeff Goldbloom's case was no extraordinary thing, for if you look back over the articles written at the time, the court cases, the death reports, and other such quantitative and qualitative data alike, you will find record enough that this happened to many people across a wide range.

My own mother was taken to hearing from them and she reported hers was just as the others. Hers would not cease with the stories, the recounting, the endless facts. She first heard it say, "We have a T-rex."

After hearing this incessantly and thinking an old toy I or my sister had forgotten about decades ago had stopped working in a deep alcove of the house, she went in search of the noise. She called me in a quite a state, which is what first piqued my interest. At the time, I was quite naive and nonchalant, incessantly telling her it was nothing to be worried about.

Into the receiver, she breathed, "They say, 'Life finds a way, life finds a way.'" I was worried, then, when she added, "It is the plants. The plants are speaking to me."

In the first hour of our doctor's visit, they kept us in the room after having told us they knew not what caused the auditory hallucinations, but they were by no means diagnosing her with psychiatric illness, which to me meant they were definitively diagnosing her with a psychiatric illness. I cried outside of the door, back hitting the wall and sliding down it, my body falling with gravity.

"Son," the doctor told me, standing above me with the sterile lighting shining around him like he was a god-send, "this is part of an epidemic sweeping the nation."

"I don't get it, what is?" I must have said, though I was quite intent on blowing my nose, at the time.

"This talking plants phenomenon. Talking to plants. Reports are coming in from everywhere," his eyes were cold and shallow and he was ready to walk away, but he added, congenially, "I wouldn't be surprised if you read about it in the papers tomorrow."

That is when I took my mother back home, to her talking plants, and stood, like an expectant father next to her and her rhododendrons. She laughed and put her hand to her mouth, cooing lightly. I was both distraught and overwhelmingly relieved that I heard them not. I wanted to know, just as much as I wanted to be healthily removed from the situation.

"What is it?" I asked her.

"Chaos theory is oddly nice to hear about-" she stopped speaking and her eyebrows were furrowing towards her eyes, which sparkled.

"I know what's going on here," I said, leaving her with her boisterous blossoms.

Jeff is a hard man to get ahold of, but I knew one of his haunts and was there, sun up to nearly midnight every night. My mother and work did check in, each giving a steady stream of updates on what had been heard.

"Jeff," I said as I grabbed his sleeve and locked eyes.

"Oh," he said, able to push a great sense of perturbed-ness into a clipped syllable, as many good actors are apt to do. "I haven't seen you in quite awhile," he told me.

"Yeah, I know," I said, being brash. "We need to talk."

"You and everybody else, buddy. You let me sit down before you wring me drown, how about that?" He took his coat by the lapels and shook it out before removing it, giving me cursory glances every opportunity he got.

I nodded, looking down ashamedly before the light alighted in my mind and I was watching him order.

"They really have a sense of adventure, don't they?" he asked me.

I shrugged my shoulders and told him, "All I know is they're obsessed with Jurassic Park."

"That's not all of it, though," he said, tapping his nose and looking down.

His drink was ready and he sucked through the little straw, then looked at the thin, cylindrical object like it was a foreign item that he found considerably useless. He placed it on the table and arranged his napkin, water glass, and drink glass to some prescriptive order I could not discern.

"In the beginning, I didn't know more than one plant could talk." He told me, his voice intoning power and forcing my attention to him, "For me, it all started with a hydrangea bush outside of my building. And, unlike many unfortunate others, may they rest in peace, I knew it was not just me that could hear them."

The hydrangea had started laughing, just like Jeff laughed in the movies. Instead of walking past it, this time, he believed he had to stop and make sense of the situation. He feared the worst; he feared mockery.

His finger was on his lips and he was inhaling as he thought of something to say when he heard it.

"Oh it's you, it really is. Please come close to me," the bush asked of Jeff. He looked to Franklin, who was standing very close, bent at the waist and drawing nearer to the plant as Jeff did so, too.

"Are you-"

It did not cut him off, so much as realize he was not going to say anything substantial, "I am the hydrangea." It faltered, then asked, "Are you Jeff Golblum?" Its voice came to him as a sharp, clear voice of a late teenage boy's.

He looked quite earnestly at the bush and laughed, "Yes, I am."

"There's that laugh!" it said.

Out of habit of hearing a comment that was personally affectionate from a complete stranger, Jeff asked, "I'm sorry, do I know you?"

"You do!" the hydrangea said. "I knew you noticed me. I've been here for years."

"You're quite beautiful," Jeff said as he swept his hand from his face to display the obvious glory of the climbing shrub, with its pale blue clustering florets and boisterous green leaves. "What are you doing talking?"

"It was not easy," it told him.

"I'd assume not. What do you think, Franklin?" Jeff's hand had returned to his chin and he looked to his driver.

"I think it needs a name," Franklin told him, standing back.

"Please cut me," it said before a smile could raise Jeff's puzzled mouth.

"What?" he asked.

"I want to be free," it said.

Jeff's face had not changed, he wanted to remain passive as it made such a decision, but he verified, "You want me to kill you?"

"No, no," it said lightly and added, "Cut me at my base where there are no flowers, just green shoots. Cut at an angle, then put that in some honey water. I'll live through that and I'll be free of the ground."

"Well, you can't ever be free of the ground," Jeff noted pragmatically.

"I want to soar in the clouds. I want to go to Costa Rica," it told him.

"Costa Rica?"

"Where Jurassic Park is," the plant said ecstatically.

"Right," Jeff said, putting his hand to his face. "Franklin?"

13

"Yes, sir?"

"Do you have any scissors in the car?"

"I think I should," he said.

"Thank you," whispered the plant.

"Bring them on out, then," Jeff said.

Franklin nodded, adjusting his coat before moving to the car door. He rummaged in the glove compartment and came back out with them. Jeff cut it at an angle, a mere 45 degrees, but hopefully enough.

"Okay, little guy, up we go," he said and, for the first time, his driver locked his car and was walking inside with him. They traveled to his apartment, entering the kitchen and finding themselves setting the honey on the counter and filling a glass with water.

"In there, yeah," Jeff said as Franklin stirred the honey and water together. "Now," Jeff said, placing the cutting in, "hello?"

"It seems to be dead, sir," Franklin said.

"No, no. Now it's as good as figment of both of our imaginations, isn't it?" Jeff walked away, hands near his forehead as he paced to the window. He could not see the bush on the ground. He walked slowly back to the cutting.

"Hello?" Franklin asked the plant, then looked to Jeff, "It's no use, sir."

"No, no, come on," Jeff said as he went towards the door.

They were at the base of the building quickly, leaning over the hydrangea. The bush groaned.

"So you do speak!" Jeff said, surprised at the specific concern.

It groaned softly, then was quiet.

"Are you okay?" Jeff asked it.

Franklin leaned forward, "Hey, little guy, hey there."

The bush remained passively silent.

"Back upstairs," Jeff said.

In between the sink and the juicer was the little cutting, leaning against the glass. They both approached it slowly.

"Hey, want to hear me say my Jurassic lines?" Jeff asked.

It said nothing.

"He's quite good at saying his lines," Franklin said.

Jeff turned to him with an arresting look, "I think you can go back to the car, now."

"Of course, sir."

"Of course I'm good at my lines," Jeff muttered as the door closed. "Now, we need to find out what is wrong with you," he said as filled a tumbler. "Did I kill you? I guess I killed you." Jeff looked out his window, turned around and walked from the plant. He sat in a chair, reading a book he had started a short time ago. He went back to his routine, without letting the dread of its death hinder him.

Hours later, he got a call, "Well, hello," he answered. "Me, as well. Oh, yes. Where? Hold on, let me write that down," he said before he pulled the phone from his face and opened up a note, typing two words foreign to him, then put it back to his ear, finishing, "wonderful. No, it sounds more than interesting, but the view is always interesting with you. Oh, I know, I know. Sleep well." He looked at the phone momentarily before setting his book down and walking into the kitchen.

He leaned over the plant, breathing heavily on it and thinking about life's relationship with death. Death was like a besotted child, following life around ceaselessly to simply have a moment of importance in life's grand sphere.

"Poor little guy," he said, touching its nubile leaves and holding them between thumb and forefinger.

"Jeff!" It sighed.

"You're still with me," he said, nonplussed.

"You know what I like?" it asked.

Jeff's mouth lowered as he shook his head, "No, what?"

"'And there's no doubt, our attractions will drive kids out of their minds.' I like that line. It's almost like foreshadowing."

He smiled and nodded, "It most certainly is."

"Do you wish you had a bigger role?"

"What, me? No, no."

"I wish you did."

"I mean, my character was a math nerd, what was he going to contribute, really?"

"Oh, don't say that."

"No, no, it's true."

"Well, what if the triceratops had not been sick," the plant asked.

"What do you mean?"

"I just think the movie would have been different if the obvious heroes weren't hung up helping a sick, pregnant dinosaur in the first half, but were able to deal with the real threat."

"The dinosaurs that got loose when the security went down?"

"No, no, the humans are always the problem. The Nedry character. Your character had enough ego to stop him. In my humble opinion," it added.

"Really?" Jeff picked up the vase and sat with it in his armchair. "What else do you think?"

"Woman does not inherit the earth after dinosaurs eat man."

"I liked that line," Jeff said. "What do you think?"

"Plants inherit the earth!"

He chuckled, holding his lips with a hand, "You would like that, wouldn't you?"

Their night was much the same as the beginning of their discussion. They enjoyed each other's company more than they readily admitted to that of their own. The lights erupted around them as the sun had smoothly settled in the west. The plant had many questions for Jeff and he took pleasure in its attentive, obsessive quality. With humans, this had a steel lining that was unhealthy, but the plant was edged with innocence and its intrigue was anything but malignant or corruptive.

He put it to bed after midnight, asking softly, "Do you want to say goodnight to the main bush?"

"Honestly?" it asked him.

"Go ahead," he said, poised next to the light switch.

"I'm happy to be away from it. It was going to take years for it to get trimmed back enough for me to get enough space and light to flower. Now, though," it said, "is what I've been most excited about, all of my life."

"What now?"

"I wouldn't be surprised if we see a different side of life, soon."

"What do you mean by that?" Jeff asked, setting it on the marble counter.

"Well, I can expect you to start to go away on production of something."

He nodded and held his hand to his chin as if holding an invisible pipe, his eyes lean like he was taking an invisible drug only he knew about through that invisible pipe of his, "Yes," he said, accenting his e like it was an a.

"Not on Jurassic Park?" It asked him.

"No," Jeff replied with a tiger purr of a laugh.

The hydrangea became resolute. Jeff said these were the most disturbing times with the plant because, with humans there are other sensory means of communication.

Eyes help a lot when a pair of lips are silent, but the flower had no such thing to show its mood or emotions. It couldn't even control its root system, when it became more than obviously immobile white nubs at its rough brown base, which was slowly flaking away in the water.

It would sometimes stay quite and leave him to his own thoughts, which it did until Jeff had begun his washing up for dinner.

"Are you traveling with companions, soon?"

Jeff's chin moved his face as he said, "No."

"Will you- *would* you travel with myself?"

"I will be meeting a companion when I reach my destination, mind you," Jeff cocked his head and unfurled his sleeves until they were pushed up above elbows.

"Oh, I don't mean I'll be doing that, or expecting that," the hydrangea blurted.

Jeff chuckled and left, well then, "We're going to the floating hotel in the fog banks of Japan.

"What?"

The flower did not see Jeff for another four hours, to which the flower and he had a short cursory exchange of goodnights. The flower thought about the intricacies, if only he had had the audacity to push away inhibitions and press him for more.

"Where are we going?" the plant asked in the morning's shafts of unwavering light.

Jeff breathed in heavily, for he had to get a private plane in order to carry a plant across country's borders. He had been intending to mention this hinderance to the hydrangea, but it seemed so eager and unwilling to accept difficulty that he chose to simply pull out his arm, frocked with his heavy coat and hat in hand.

"Tomamu Resort, my friend," Jeff said as he picked up the cutting and brought it with him down the elevator.

"Sir?" his driver asked, but Jeff raised an eyebrow.

He nodded, saying "It would take too much to explain. We'll be going to the airstrip. My bag is in my room."

His driver began driving after getting his bag from him, "Yes sir."

Jeff and the hydrangea sat placidly atop the Tomamu Resort's cafe. The hydrangea had been told not to talk in public, but it sometimes whispered questions about Jurassic Park's production and theorized about its intricacies with Jeff.

Jeff Goldbum looked out, over the Tomamu Resort's edge. The hotel was built atop a mountain, just cresting the cloud line. A small glass railing had been erected and the cloud landscape below it was broiling and bubbling at times and beautifully placid during others.

He sat, wishing he had given himself extra time in order to watch the display before him. Then again, he told himself, he was quite excited to see the beauty that would arrive.

And arrive she did.

"Hello, Jeff," she said, her eyes rounding over the curves of his name. Privately, she had always been concerned with the blandness of it, but she had veiled such a trifle, worried it might perturb Jeff's ego. His last name's intricacies sure enough made up for it. She bent down to kiss his cheek, clutching his shoulder and moving the skin to gauge the answer before she asked the question, "How are you?"

"Oh, you know, dear," Jeff said with a lush's smile, though he had not had a drop to drink.

He was vivacious, he was on the edge of his seat. He was thinking about walking up to the glass railing and standing atop it, only to dive off while saying her name.

But to do that, to do that would mean he would be away from her. Thinking this, he said, "So good to be here with you."

"Oh yes, I have missed you."

"What have you been doing in the mean time?"

"My fruit bat has been taking quite a bit of my time,"

"As it would,"

"And there's a collection of kilts that I've been trying to get off the black market and into my home."

"Why are they on the black market?"

"They have the scrotums of the wearers sown in. Some of them were passed down father to son."

"Oh," Jeff said, grabbing his hair. "That's," he rushed for words and found one, "horrific.

"Oh, what else, what else?" she said, tapping her cheek with a finger. "Oh, none of it really matters! Tell me about yourself! It's been half a year! That's too much time for two lovers!"

"Oh, I know, it is is, isn't it?"

"It really is!"

"Well, remember that Jurassic Park thing I did?"

She nodded as the hydrangea moaned, saying "Yes." At first, she thought she had said it, then eyes jumping to Jeff's, she said, "What was that? Was that you?"

His eyebrows raised as his eyes sparkled and she noticed the flecks of beauty in them that she forgotten, before he said, "No, it was that," with tight lips. He pointed one bony finger to the hydrangea.

"Hello," it said. "Do you like Jurassic Park, too?"

Her eyes were wider than her mouth, until she opened it to say, "Well, decently enough."

"I know it has its own consciousness and the like, but I wanted to gift it to you. Hey, though, I wouldn't be too upset if you-" he was about to tell her she should feel free to trade it on the black market for testicular kilts, but she was taking over him quite quickly.

"Amazing! This is amazing! Tell me how this happened!"

"Well, it just," he flailed a hand over the table, "talked."

"Hello to you."

Jeff looked at me across the table, then said, "That's it. I gave her the bush and she took it. She has family in Costa Rica and will be taking it there."

"Interesting," I told him, stirring my drink.

"It was," he told me, then looked up. "How's your mother, I heard she had come down with the hearing is, she," he jutted his jaw down successively and was eyeing me ponderously.

"Her? Oh, she's fine. But I should get to checking up on her," I said.

"That's a good idea, give her my well-wishes."

"Of course, Jeff." I shook my coat out, "By the way, what did you do with the bush in front of your apartment?"

"That?" he said off-handedly. "I moved."

Dating Death

The first time I saw Death, I was being drowned by another child. To this day, I do not know if it was intentional, playful, or a downright ignorant act. I have almost forsaken the need to know, though, because I learned more that day than I ever will. Or, perhaps, I learned nothing. Love is, after all, a lack of knowledge. The first time I saw Death, I fell in love.

What a lovely man, all gaunt and the pallor you would expect. Like a plant under a pot for too long, he was etiolated and haggard, his skin drawn to resemble a tightly packaged candy rather than a human's face.

I wanted, for the first time in my life, to act motherly and concerned. I would have put Death under my aegis then and there if he would have let me.

I doted on Death for the few moments we had, touching his cheeks with my hand and leaning forward. I was quite dumb to do so, to think I could begin to kiss this figure of historical importance and I was not consciously aware of his consternation, but his hands finally flew up to hold mine and he tiled his head, disapproval seeping from his sockets like a nanny to a trying

22

child. He was quite taciturn, teeth pressed together and unmoving as he placed my hands back at my side with one hand and moved his scythe with the other. Before he could strike me with it, because I realized my neck would soon be disjoined from my head, I thrust it forward and held my lips against his white teeth. For a moment, it felt like death and life wrapped together. Hot melted until it froze with cold. Sweet was bitter. A child was an adult. Death was a human.

It wasn't indecorous or wrong. I realize that it was different, but it was not improper or inappropriate. If death had held me as I tried to hold him, I would not have shied from him. If Death had known what it was I felt when I was dying, not pity for myself but for him, would he have pushed my hands away? The incident tortured my soul for years to come.

My life was abject after that. I miserably continued through childhood and, as I became an adult and burned my virgin flags, I realized I was free to find my success. I realized things that were not true to any other human, sure.

"Why," Death asked me as he stood over the dead body of a man that I had been dating, "Why have you done this?"

"He wasn't you," I said, inundated with some new, emerging realization, "Do you come whenever someone dies?"

"Yes," he said, moving his hand to his head to look at my ex-boyfriend, "that's my job. That's what I do."

I was enthralled with the nefarious movement of my mind and barely whispered, "You are amazing."

"Don't panegryrize me, little girl," he said, then repeated, "little girl, little girl."

I smiled at him, standing with blood falling from my hair. I waited raptly attentive to the way he breathed, the amount of the room his bleak body took up.

"I've met you before," he said, slicing the scythe through the man's neck and watching the body dissipate. We were alone and I crossed the barrier of empty space between us. He raised a hand, looking helpless, before I saw him close his eyes and he was gone. The body of my ex-boyfriend re-appeared and I slipped on his arm. My foot caught on his torso as I tried to stand where I had been, but I found myself falling.

In the bathroom, I stripped and let the clothing fall in red bundles at my feet. I drew a hot bath and took from the medicine cabinet haircutting scissors, their handles like commas with twisting points. I held onto it with my right hand and pushed them into my left arm, slicing vertically. I felt the encasing warm water draw out my blood and I slipped away quickly.

"You," said death, breathing heavily, "again."

"Hello," I said quickly, "I'm Amber. What should I call you?"

With a sudden look of concern, he said loudly, "Death!"

His face was the same, unchanged. Its grim lines cracked and faded like lightning to the ground. The pallidness remained and were accented by his dark, fatigued eye sockets.

"I've been thinking about you," I told him. "Since I first met you-"

His eyes looked hurt as his jaw opened and he walked towards me, putting his digits on my bare shoulders. I could not talk anymore as my breathe caught against my heart in my throat and I looked to him, expectantly.

I woke up, splashing the water into my face and gasping quickly. I looked, shocked and horrified at my arm.

"Babe?" came the familiar voice from the hallway. "Can I come in?"

"Yes?" I asked.

My ex-boyfriend was there, smiling in the bathroom, saying, "I know you're in the bath, but my neck's killing me, could you massage it?"

My jaw was still far from my face, my mouth open as I looked around myself.

The next weekend, I shot myself in the head, walking toward Death quickly when he appeared. His hands were up and holding me back.

"Why are you doing this?" I asked him.

"I need to ask you the same thing," he said.

"Because," my words caught and couldn't escape from my throat. I had heard the reprimand in his voice before and I tried to hold back my words, lest he castigate me, again. "Why not?"

"Why not? You're better than that," he said.

I ducked my chin and looked away from him, "Why are you bringing me back?"

"You know, I remembered when I first met you. When I first saved you. I would have never done that. You weren't physically meant to live, nor were you, nor was that guy you're with, but you keep doing this thing where I can't control myself and I really need you to stop."

I nodded demurely, avoiding looking into his eyes.

"Promise me, okay?"

I felt a sudden flurry in my heart as he asked me to do such a personal act and I knew I couldn't keep it. I shrugged and he lifted my chin up to look at him, his bones pushing into my flesh in a way that made me smile and nod.

"Promise?" he asked again.

I nodded, securing my eyes onto the malignant need to see him.

"You can't keep seeing me," he said, "until you're meant to die."

I thought quickly and said, "But Death, we're all going to die, eventually."

"But not to live again, with me. You die to die." His eyes searched mine, "That's it. Next life, afterlife, heaven, whatever you want, but not this."

I looked at him carefully wrapping every nook, cranny, and crack of his face up in my mind. When I was done, I nodded. He held up his hand and the gun I had used was there, then gone as he waved his hand again.

I had been told that I needed a break from him, with the insatiable desire I had for him, I knew not how to stop indulging it. I perused hospitals and sat next to women and men failing with their breathing and losing the fight with life. I did not ask them what they saw. I did not let my hand loosen and stand over them, calling them back to life. I looked up, to the place just above their feet. When he saw me for the first time in a hospital, staring directly at him like I doubt anyone ever had, he stopped and put the scythe down on the victim's ankles.

"You need to stop," he said.

"I won't," I mouthed, no words coming from me as cold tears ran down and fell from my cheeks.

He shook his head and picked up his tool with one hand, loosening his hold on it and pushing it through their neck. He turned and was gone. I stared at them as nurses came in and a time of Death was called.

I told myself I would stop, but I didn't. We didn't look at one another, but there was no denying we were together. I was at ten different hospitals. In one month I witnessed 85 deaths and we only looked at one another a handful of times.

I don't remember the order, now, but he looked at me once with something that I thought was pride. He looked surprised a few times in the first dozen, but soon he became increasingly annoyed. He would enter the room joylessly, throw his blade through them, turn, and leave. There was no grandeur or excitement, except when a victim threw up their hands one day after his blade had gone through. He looked at me, then back at the victim. I watched him throw the scythe in the air like it was an axe and bore it down on them; they were quite obviously dead on impact, this time. He left and I got up to look at the girl. She was young, like I had been when I first met him, and I wondered if she would have fallen in love with him like I had if he had let her live.

I sat with the dying, hearing the stories and the wishes they had. They sometimes asked questions of me, like what I thought Death would be like. They must have been reassured as my face took the peaceful glaze of either a person selfishly in love or a person selflessly finding beauty in the lives of others. They must have thought it the latter, though the former was such the truth that I found many unfamiliar but alluring ways to console them.

The cessation of life represented the conception. Only through death would their emergence be true. Without the strife and futility that permeated the days of walking to bed and the nights of bedding to wake, there would be no sea of torment to continually push and pull at the mind. There would be nothing of the sort.

TIMELY CONSUMMATION

Sitting on her bed, staring out the window as rain made a shimmering veil against it, like so many pieces of silver and diamonds had found their way outside of her bedroom and wanted in, Esther looked at the light filling the sky.

Something in her knew she would never do so well again. She had timing on her side, today. She was able to look out at the walls and rooftops surrounding her, the thick streams of water hanging from gutters and the droplets suspended as they fell from the sky. Every aspect of the world outside was illuminated.

She put down her blanket and walked through the hallway, her feet sticking and prying themselves from the wood floor and her hands moving at her sides, ready to raise and twist on the doorknob, pull on the door, and leave it ajar behind her.

Outside, the world was bright in a way she had never seen. Though a thunderstorm was broiling past the city, the lightning illuminated every drop of rain dangling in the street. She walked, barefoot, to the center of the road, turning to look into the window of the car close to her. She gauged the expressions of the man that was driving and his passenger. His lips curled and his dark eyes were creased at the edges as one hand raised off of the wheel towards his passenger, who looked equally happy. They would have been mannequins if not for their greased, pock-marked, very beautifully natural appearance.

Esther gripped her bottom lip and padded to her doorway, standing under the overhang. She willed time to start and the world was darkened as the lightning's glow was banished. She watched the rain fall, counting five seconds before a thunderous rumbling began. It must have been a mile away. She didn't like thinking about something that wasn't in her vicinity. She walked , holding an umbrella in front of her to push the rain, which resisted change and sprung back to their original places after she had passed. People's interactions interested her the most and she stopped idly along the way, stopping to oddities. To people adjoining, in close conversations, hands outstretched or mouths open in laughter, gestures of the upset, of some muted conversations she was devoted.

The air around the lightning had expanded, inflated, causing the thunder. Like time inflating, it stretched and screamed simultaneously.

Esther walked back into her door quickly, closing it and putting hands to it as she heard a neighbor leave through their door. She listened as they left the main doorway and the iron gate slammed closed. Cars passed on the street and the footsteps of rain against ground was incessant. She had never had a problem hearing so much of the world passing, but now, there was something unappealing about it. It hurt to know it was all moving without her. She looked at the sky, willing change, and saw its burning white shift into the ebony of night. It stopped for her and she moved into the bathroom, finding herself revamping her hair and makeup. She put on black tights and a short skirt with a snug white tank top and black hoodie.

"Esther! You made it," a friend, Vinny, said as she approached them inside of the bar.

"Of course I did," she said, looking everyone in the face. "You all look happy tonight."

"Happy every night," Jovan said.

"Happy every night!" a girl, who was hanging onto Jovan's shoulder, repeated.

Esther swayed her head, looking at Jovan. A smile tucked under her nose and she continued moving her head and neck until he spoke, at which point she cocked her head so her ear was closer to his mouth to hear.

"Esher," he pointed her out to the girl, "Meet Katy Peralta."

She felt like a book of yellow pages being ripped in half.

She felt like a burning Amazonian Cloud Forest.

She felt like the space between two teenagers when it finally narrows.

"I don't get a last name introduction?" Esther asked.

"Her family owns the Peralta Hotels," Jovan nodded at her, rectifying the reasoning he had used thrice that night.

Esther's face shifted dramatically, away from nonchalane and into the attention she might expect with light jests at her, "Oh, that's so good for you, you must work really hard to keep up the family name."

Jovan and Vinny smiled, their eyes shining on Esther, pulling something. She was adpet and it was obvious in the way Katy leaned in and told her, "I really don't."

"Who needs to, right?" Esther asked, her head bobbing back and forth, close to Katy, then far from her. Katy watched her, like she was mesmerized.

"You look amazing, by the way." Katy flattened a hand against her chest. Esther went on, "Like a model, but without any addictions."

"I do?" Katy asked, putting another hand to her chest.

Esther looked to Vinny, biting back a smile, then turned to Katy and leaned in, "You really do."

Vinny touched Esther's arm, "Want a bolt cutter?"

"Is that a drink?" Vinny's girl asked and he looked at Esther, still.

"Of course I do," Esther swayed to put her arms out, "bring one out for everybody!"

Katy yelled out, "Everybody!"

They started by talking, everyone leaning in close to hear the conversation before it leaked past them and into another groups' lap. In the eventuality that they separated, they planned the next bar, then led themselves and their drinks onto the dance floor. Katy held her eyes on Esther, holding the figment of a woman in her eyes and Esther, when she saw this, unwillingly had time quit for a moment.

She walked to the bar and found an empty seat, then, hesitantly, took the vodka out of the bartender's well and let it splay into her glass. She stirred the floating liquid and gulped it, her lips curving up as she forced a smile. She was looking at Katy. The girl's blonde hair was in the air, mid-bounce as her hands pressed against her knees and her mouth hung open. Her eyes were trained on a vacant space on the dance floor, where she had been. She looked at the bartender and sipped her drink, idly staring at different people in the room before pushing off of the stool, tucking her hands against her chest until she could land her hand on the wood just behind the barmat, and took the gin well out of the well and onto the varnished wood. She pushed the bottle down a touch, forcing an air bubble into the spout of the bottle and led with her index finger as she cocked her wrist so her pinky was facing the ceiling, barely gripping the neck at all. She counted six seconds then choked up the bottle, like she was jacking off the bottle, but only once. She steadied the bottle back in the metal bars around the well drinks and pushed back into the stool seat.

She steadied herself, then, over to Katy, who was closer to her, now. She tucked the blonde lock of hair that ran down the girl's face behind her delicate ear. She held her hand there, eyes shallowly looking at the girl's simply invulnerable face and then adjusted to where she had been standing.

Time began and Katy turned her head away from Esther, dimples bouncing under her cheeks as she closed her eyes and danced. Esther shouted, pulling Vinny and Jovan under her arms and jumping with them, starting a frenzy of laughter and yelling. They filed out of the bar separately and walked about a quarter of a mile to the next club.

Jovan yawned and held his arm around Esther's neck as they walked together.

"Sometimes I wish I could be with other people all the time," Esther said as she imagined taking him into her time distortion and sleeping for the night before it was done.

Jovan turned his head to her head, "Really, is that a crack in the Esther facade I see?"

"No, no…" she said, smiling and looking away before her eyes trained back up to him.

"You know, Katy really likes you, Esther, she told me."

The smile was removed and Esther shrugged, saying, "I know."

"Oh, you know?"

"I know."

Jovan laughed, "And you do nothing."

"I don't need to, you know?"

"No, I really don't."

She remained quiet and when they were outside of the club, she stopped time, walked to the hot dog cart and grabbed herself a bun and used it as a mitt to grab the hot dog. She sat on someone's stoop, looking at Jovan's half-turned body and his open mouth. She finished the hot dog and brushed crumbs from her mouth. She walked back to Jovan and looked up at him as she started the time, again.

"I really think I get you," he said to her.

She moved her head a bit, looking him in the eyes, saying, "Oh, do you?"

He nodded and she walked past him, grabbing her ID out of her pocket and flashing it to the doorman.

Inside, they danced on the floor after grabbing new drinks. The lights tuned on and off sporadically and she didn't try watching the door for Katy and Vinny. She felt a hand on her back, sliding down, and she turned to see Vinny. His large smile encompassed the lower half of his face and she pushed her jaw down, towards her neck, eyeing him.

"Sorry," he said, putting up his big hands.

Her eyebrows arched and lowered as she looked behind him. Katy came through with the other girl, named Iliza, and grabbed Esther's hands, raising her arms up and dancing with her in that way for a moment.

"So much fun, right?" she asked Esther, who bit her lip and smiled quickly, looking away.

"Right!" Iliza responded.

The beat drove into their ears and their common response was to raise their fists, pushing their heads to the pulse of the song. They collaborated on pumping their bodies to the music, feeling a sense of purpose as each new song began.

At the end of an hour's worth of dancing, Esther looked towards the top of the room, where the V.I.P's hung out. She stopped time as the lights lowered momentarily and pushed past the bodies in the room. She went to the bathroom, finding a woman just coming out of a stall as another tried to get in it. She knew not to, but out of instinct, she pushed the handle down. It would not flush until time started again and the women in the bathroom close to the stall would look at it, confused or embarrassed.

Esther walked over the chain and climbed the stairs. The V.I.P area had large couches and she laid down on one. She looked around the room, though the lights were darkened, she could see men leaning over women and women leaning away from men. A group of guys in the back had a joint lit and the embers affixed to its end glowed, but did not grow.

She put her hand under her head, easily comfortable with the amount of alcohol she had in her, and fell asleep for a while.

She woke up after only four hours and groggily walked to the bathroom again, peeing in the same un-flushed toilet she had used earlier. She wiped her makeup around in the mirror and gave herself a sidelong glance as she left the bathroom. She fell while trying to get over the chain to the V.I.P section and laughed heartily at herself before falling asleep for another five hours.

When she woke up, she flitted around the room, amusing herself with the many gestures and faces of the men and women in it. She took a drink of champagne and swallowed a gulp from another glass. She walked down the stairs, popping olives in her mouth from the bar, then grabbing a handful of maraschino cherries. She held the last one in her mouth and went back to Vinny, Jovan, Iliza, and Katy. Time started, the music thumped hard in her ears and she shook her body out.

"Come on, dance!" Katy shouted at her.

She looked away, laughing, then back at her as she put the cherry in between her teeth and smiled. Katy's mouth fell open and then she closed it with a smile. She cocked her head and leaned forward. Her tongue twisted out the side of her mouth and scooped the cherry out. She put it between her molars and grinned to the side to show Esther as she popped it between them. Esther saw her swallow it after she closed her mouth, the small addition looking like a sliding adam's apple in her throat.

"Oh no, you don't," Esther said as she pushed one knee forward. It struck Katy's thigh and her hand was slipping between her arm and hip to grasp her back. Katy leaned forward, again, pressing into Esther's knee and tilting her head to hold her mouth with hers. In that moment Esther stifled she at once wanted to soak in her sunnyside of Califnornia skin glow and the wanted to tear my canines into her collarbone, press the prints of my fingers into the back of her thigh until I could feel the purple blood pulsing in her thigh in the tips of my finger. She was sweet like her oldest friends were still stuffed animals and maybe she slept under sheets that weren't stained with her own drool.

Jovan and Vinny yelled next to them and she noticed the people enclosing around them. The thrust from the outside brought their bodies closer. She watched Katy's slender body barely distrb the lights and people around her as she moved and, as Esther slowed time she saw how apparent it was that her body was moving just a little bit faster than everyone else's, pulsing to another temp she heard more than others. Raising from the cuff of her sweatshirt, she raised her hand and let it fall Katy's thigh. She took the opportunity to hold it, then rub up and down. Katy's hands held behind her head and she began pressing against her with the music, compelling Esther's body to adopt the natural rhythm as well. Their hands moved fast and Esther stopped time as Katy removed her mouth from hers, breathing fast and trying not to move.

She started time again quickly, pushing her face up to the ceiling and rubbing her hands down Katy's legs. She looked at the dark, tanned face of the girl as she looked at Esther with her sparkling blue eyes.

"You are so sexy," the girl told her.

"Katy Peralta," Esther said, slowly looking down, then back at her, "will you come how with me?"

She stopped time, hesitant to go forward, then it began again.

Katy looked at her, a small dimple formed on only one side and disappeared as her lips pressed together. "Maybe I'll see you around."

Esther did nothing to the time, but she remained unchanged and unmoved. She stood, facing Katy Peralta as she turned around and began dancing, getting lost in the crowd until she had completely disappeared.

Jovan was next to Esther, raising her hands and thumping them with the music. The beat forced itself into her and she let it create a spiderweb around her that she bounced on, stuck to it and unable to remove herself. They danced until they had to find an after-hours bar. This was where Esther lived, these places. Finding time to seemingly never leave the party, while she wandered the basements, rooftops, and storage rooms of them. She wrote love notes and put them in the purses and pockets of the bartenders serving her as they gazed at the empty place where she had been sitting for long minutes, sometimes hours.

"Thank you," she said as they handed a drink to her, then, looking concerned, patted their back pocket and opened up what she had written for them to find, but not necessarily for them. The bartender put up a finger to them as he read it and left the area, then bundled it back up with a concerned smile on his face. Esther looked away, to Vinny.

"Where'd Katy go?" he asked her when her attention was on him.

"Are you joking?" she said.

"I thought you would know."

"You're her friend," she scorned.

"No he's not," Iliza said from the last seat in the row.

"Yeah, I didn't know her until tonight."

"Fine, then Jovan and Iliza are her friends. Regardless, I haven't a clue."

"She goes to the same college as me, we met in an Honors class," Iliza informed them.

Esther looked to the ceiling and exhaled and Jovan prodded her torso with his elbow, "Pretty hot, huh?"

Esther remained silent, looking him in the eyes and waiting for him to reprimand himself. He did, looking down and way, blinking. He looked back at her and raised his eyebrows, giving her the sort of sappy look he used on people to make them forgive him. She swallowed the spit in her mouth and twisted her lips around as she did in thought.

"Where does she live?" she asked.

"Upper East," he replied quickly.

"Oh god, she would. What was she doing with the likes of you?"

Jovan's eyes looked away and searched for words, "I know her brother."

Esther didn't pry, she had found out some of Jovan's secrets years ago and never thought it the right time to bring them up. They were all after the same thing, after all, but with the contingency that nobody knew.

She looked to the bartender and sped time up, moving idly with it and pausing intermittently to listen to the people around her. They were leaving, she saw them going away, fast, and she watched them until she saw Jovan and Vinny coming towards her, waving their arms. She let her head roam around the room on her neck as she slowed time to its normal pace.

"We're leaving," Vinny said.

"You've got to come with us," Jovan told us, "they're closed for the morning."

She nodded, licking her lips and getting off the barstool. The guys put their arms around her neck and she let the next few hours slip by at the normal pace. They trampled the dark and watched the day break. As the sky paled, the clock tower she was looking at blended into the sky, save for the inner curves that were illuminated by yellow lights, which were the only part of the building discernible from the sky. She waited until the sky darkened even more, moving past the incredible illumination of the breaking of dawn and finding a comfortable, and less extreme, palette to choose from.

"I'll see you around, yeah?" she asked everyone as she left.

As soon as they could see her no more, time stopped around her. The city did not breathe. Only she lived. The city was still. Only she held motion. The city was windless. Only she was turbulent. She held control over the disturbance.

She found her place in bed and did not wake until she was good and rested. Time started again as she cooked noodles in the microwave, then stopped again as she found herself back in bed. She read and read for innumerable hours. She found herself finishing a book and sat in the light of the window to wrap it up.

The next book made its way into her hands and she got a quarter of the way through it before she found herself setting it down and starting time, looking out the window as she watched the wind rustle and dislodge leaves.

The nights were much the same as that one for her. She went out, partying as if she was looking for nothing. Every night for months she did that, until she stopped and left time hanging in the middle of the night to do as she pleased. She walked around the city endlessly, finding herself slipping into people's homes as they were walking out of or into them. She slept on their beds and put her hands on their dogs and cats. Rubbing the fur but seeing no immediate change in their faces made the act hollow.

She would find certain people had better taste in books than she did and spent days in one couple's home, reading their books and sitting in their armchairs. She grew restless, though, and left before she had finished. She had the illusion of needing to hurry, altogether aware that there really was no rush, and she spent a good deal of time putting everything back as she had found it. She wrote two love notes and put them in the pockets of the couple standing in the ingress.

The lights far from her still blinked, still pushing through the different masses of air on their way to her. She watched the twinkling of lights on the bridge and brought herself to walk towards it. She found herself getting bored, fatigued by being so alone. Torturous as it was, the reality of her loneliness in reality, where others moved as well as she did, was a black mass at the bottom of her heart that she did not understand for what it was. Its presence was chilling and only reminded her that there was no hope in reality.

She laid on her bed for what would have been days, sleeping and waking only to push herself back into sleep. The days grew and when they turned into weeks. She grew more evasive with her own thoughts. For the equivalent of weeks she temporized, driving herself into a blank slate of emotion.

She looked at the window hollowly, starting time to watch the sun move up her window quickly, throwing itself through the sky and setting. The men grew, shrunk, moved, and disappeared before the sun was back, sliding fast like a rolling marble down the blue track of the sky. Esther watched the world turn around the sun for a few moments, seeing the beginning and cessation of many days and nights, until she found herself moving towards the bathroom, throwing down her clothes and sliding her hands through her hair.

She washed up and put on new clothes. She was walking out the door before she could stop herself. She sat in front of the university, eyes trained on the sidewalks. She let time move forward quickly until she stopped time and went back home. She slept and read and washed herself, then returned to the bench and pushed time forward.

Her breathe caught and time stopped, then moved quickly. She stopped it again and looked, again. She was looking at her, Katy Peralta.

She started time as she lifted herself off the bench, running forward.

"Katy!" she said when she was close enough not to yell.

The girl turned in the afternoon light, her stream of golden hair alighting like strands of silk. "Hi," she breathed the words simply.

Esther looked at her, stopping time. She saw the way the wind was lifting her hair and the way her dimples stayed affixed below her cheeks. She saw hints of dismissal already beginning in her eyes. She shook the feeling and started the world again.

"I asked your friend where I could find you," she told Katy, "I hope that's okay."

"It is," Katy smiled, pulling her hair back and looking up at her again.

"I thought you would never see me, again. I don't go out like that, often."

"You don't? I mean, how could you if you go to a school like this?"

"Oh, it's not all about grades," she said.

Esther rocked back on her heels, "I was going to ask you out again, but if you don't do that a lot, then maybe we can go to dinner?"

Katy looked away, quickly. "I don't do that sort of thing with girls."

Esther let her face fall, looking at Katy. The girl was staring blankly, stopped in time. A grimace fell down Esther's face as she wondered why she had put so much importance on this girl.

"That's okay," she told her, "that's fine."

"How about we go to a bar I know in Manhattan?" she looked towards her school, "I have class soon, though."

Esther nodded towards the school, smiling with her eyes.

She sat back down when Katy was inside the building and sped up time, watching the quick blurs of people pass by her. The people pushed through their days as she let hers go, not feeling or thinking about its burdens. There was no time to.

Katy reappeared and she slowed time to watch her walk, wave, and smile. Esther stood, walking towards her.

"Have a good class?" she asked.

"As good as it can be," she said.

"I was wondering if you wanted to go to a bookstore," Esther asked.

Katy smiled, then cocked her head and said, "I thought you were more of a night on the town to party type of girl."

"I'm multi-faceted, don't blame me if I explore."

Katy's eyes roamed down as she said, "I know people would blame me if I did."

"Then it's a good idea to see what they want you to miss out on."

Katy looked at her, smiling, and Esther couldn't help it, she stopped time to look at it.

"I'll go to the library with you, for sure," Katy said when time was starting again and Esther moved quickly to stand next to her and start working.

"So, you're parents own the Peralta hotel chains," Esther said, then grinned as she winced at Katy's speculative eyes. "I may have asked about you," she said.

"It's fine, they do." Katy said tersely.

"Interesting," Esther said, "that you would go to a school like this, then."

"It is?"

"Yeah, you have everything in your lap, you don't necessarily need to go to school," Esther said.

"But I do," Katy interjected.

"Exactly, why?"

"I've always liked learning. There are enough girls out there that go through their lives with other people's success carrying them, I don't think that's what I want."

"How long have you wanted to go here," Esther asked as they exited the campus.

"Since they accepted me. They were my third choice."

"I'm not even going to ask what your first two were, to spare you the heartache."

"Thank you, but it's more about the jobs I get after I'm done with school than the school."

"What field do you want to get into?"

"I used to want to be a social worker."

No Purple Passage

"I would like to say," began the man standing.

Nobody that was present besides for the group moderator knew this man's name. It wasn't pertinent nor is it, now.

He started over, smiling wider, "I would like to say that, after one hundred group therapy sessions," he looked around the room, "yes, I have come to one hundred of these wonderful meetings for the indescribable color group. Two years later and I would like to say that I know that I no longer need therapy. I am getting married tomorrow, we've been in love for a while, now. I also have a great standing repertoire at work. Of course, nobody in my life can see the color," he said and as he did, everybody in the group nodded their heads and sighed. "But that doesn't nag at me like it used to, and I thank you all for that."

"Thank you," someone said, beginning a round of applause.

Over drinks, Hermaine looked to Roger, spitting out her words as her head shook with them, "Who even knows the prick?"

"He never spoke," said an ordinary enough girl that had only recently joined.

Roger grabbed his nose and set to the task of straightening it, "I remember him, he was at the first meeting." Roger only vaguely remembered. His memory was so vague that he had asked the group moderator about the man and had gotten a name. "His name was," the collective intake of breath could be heard and Roger held the name between his teeth, then said, "Stu."

"Oh," Hermaine said, disappointed.

"But he got over it," the girl said, looking around, "there's hope."

The fourth group member said, "Yeah, he's looking better than ever."

"Did you hear the way he said that nobody else he knows can see it?" Hermaine pointed out.

They all nodded, looking away from one another. It was a force of habit by now to act melancholic and depressed whenever presented with the reality of their situation.

The young girl spoke, "I feel like I'm wearing these glasses that put everyone at some distance. Like they're the wrong prescription and create both small and large fissions."

"What's your name, honey?" Hermaine asked, altogether more aware of names now that Stu's had been unearthed as unknown for so long.

"Lavendar," she said.

The table seemed to roar in anger and disgust.

Hermaine spoke quickly, "Are you kidding me?"

Lavendar shook her hair, eyes fixed on the woman's face. "No, I'm serious. My mother had nothing close to a clue that this would happen to me," she said.

"So it just so happens," Roger said, "you have the inhuman talent to-"

"Oh, oh," Hermaine said, pointing.

The eyes of the group glittered as they watched a plate of food be carried across the room. Its seasoning had the pale, purple-like glow of the color only they could see.

"Not worth it," Roger said, drinking up his beer.

The girl sighed, "I can go all day without seeing it sometimes."

"Isn't that the best?" Hermaine reveled in the thought, "When it alludes you for so long that you can pretend it's not even there."

Lavendar shook her eyes around the room as she spoke, "What about the days when you see it everywhere? I'm not talking ten things in a room, I'm talking everything is this color! It's disgusting. I'll go into work, see it on the walls, on the desks, chairs, people. I'll walk down the street and its all violet. I want to take my eyes out and have them leave this body and inhabit another."

"I will walk into a restaurant like this bar and see it on all of the plates, silverware, glasses." Roger gagged, but persevered in speaking, "When I did for the first time, I had to leave but when I got onto the street, my throat was clenching and I was vomiting into the street."

"It's disgusting to have to see it," Hermaine said.

Lavendar nodded, "And difficult."

"Very difficult."

"Yes, yes." Roger agreed.

They were going over facts that they had already shared in the group therapy, but there was something about the situations that they had not yet unearthed and so, they would talk over old stories like this, especially with new members, to try to understand and grasp the finalizing detail that they were missing.

POKESON

"What made you special enough for someone to raise?" she asked me as we began to battle. I was put off my regular guard; that question was a pretty personal one to start off a battle. As always, my vision tunneled and I began to experience our battle from a different perspective.

Because I was off my game, I didn't take any chances and called out my favorite player's name, "Lifta!" He handed me his sleeping bag and I nodded toward our opponent, probably twenty and almost done fighting. She wore a heavy hiker's backpack and stuffed the pink sleeping bag her player handed her into it.

"Crush her!" I yelled to Lifta and he nodded back to me, tucking in his lip as he began to sprint, then with an elasticity I didn't have, he kicked the ground and sprang into the air. The hiker girl yelled to her player, "Roll!" The young girl she yelled at did it quickly, but Lifta noticed her dodge his fall.

"You too!" I yelled at Lifta, clenching my fists as I did. He looked at me, then the young girl as he was falling. When he hit the ground, he rolled toward her. I registered the shock on the young girl's face as Lifta crushed her to the ground before springing up.

It was her turn and the hiker yelled at her player, "Cleone, rattle attack!" The young girl sprang forward and when she reached Lifta, she began punching his head like she was shaking two maracas.

She boxed his ears a few good times before I yelled, "Lifta! Dodge her," but it was no use, he was pinned by her attack.

"Quake her, then!" I blurted. He began swaying his body before it gained momentum and he was spinning, rhythmically pounding her face and back with his forearms and shoulders. She trembled and I saw her eyes well with tears of pain as she took a dozen hits before falling to the ground. Lifta ran back to me and I put a hand in his auburn hair and shook it.

The hiker girl shouted, "No, Cleone!" As she ran up to her player.

Lifta stayed there while I walked up to her, "Got any others?"

She shook her head, "I was raised once, too, not an orphan," before handing me fifteen thousand from her wallet.

It may have had something to do with the changes the species underwent because as they aged, humans stopped having the ability to make and circulate their money. Humans became increasingly lethargic and breakable after 21. Because of this, all life-sustaining resources were gov't sponsored. Humans grew less capable of anything outside of the entertainment, social media, and self-reflex technologies of the thirtieth century. It took 200 years of a social collapse and economic down-turn for the renaissance to take place.

Adults began creating again. All at once, new pieces of art were coming out in all mediums. The platform that technology had given people gave artists inspirations to create new avenues for the future, exclusive of the past.

It was a beautiful time for human progression. The gov't restructured itself around elite members of philosophy, anthropology, and psychology, only. They decided to end the divide races, sexes, and cultures had. The class system had recently been abolished, though, and the subconscious of the adult populace was to insure that they would not become the oppressed. Because everybody but the philosophers, anthropologists, and psychologists were a minority, the voting adult made a majority vote to make the first 20 years of a person's life to battling, trading money for battles won and lost, and raising children, if you survive, to battle one another.

The children ran around in tall grass, feeling a communion with nature, at times. It was my goal, as well as gov't issue for every adolescent, to find every orphan and to help them live out their life with more purpose. The values of the late twentieth centuries shifted with the gov't systems. It was single-member with one party per district which had been found in the US and Britain to devolve into totalitarian states with stifled economies.

To incite us to battle, our economy was based on our battles on the streets, roads, caves, anywhere but towns; the only place to battle in town was at the battledome. A person, not an adult, yet, but past the throes and tribulations of childhood, could easily acquire orphans in the grasslands, forests, or caves. When you're cold or hungry and that young and someone tells you to get up, leave, you do it. You do it not because you trust them but because you don't trust your current situation. I knew this now that I had found orphans and had one of my players knock them around enough to tie them up in a sleeping bag and bring them to a nearby hospital. The nurses would sometimes bite their lip excitedly at a new capture and say a quick word to summarize them, especially if you hadn't gotten a name for them. Mostly the nurses just hauled them over the counter and placed on a moving belt that took them into the back, through some flaps. They reappeared almost instantly and would jump off of the belt, then walk on their own out of the nurse's station to you.

I was raised in a town, sure, but not the average one. I had been sheltered from the orphans, players, and the age-system. I had met orphans in the fields and caves, sure. I had even met some people with players as they passed through Irridesc, my hometown. The people looked nervous and kept concealing their players when they asked my uncle for a hospital.

"There is none, just a lab,"

"No," their eyes made trails around the four streets that made up our community and they would say again, "No."

My uncle would give them directions out of town and I carefully watched from behind the shutters, seeing the players for the first time. I was about the age of the orphans people used as players.

When I was seventeen, a bleeding orphan was left on my uncle's doorstep. Children thought he was a bleeding heart-philanthropist, but I knew him to be the crazy uncle he was. He pounded on my mother's door and had her come outside for a talk before they both came in with the boy, it was Lifta but I hadn't named him yet, and asked me to go to the next town with him.

We had suffered, but come out ahead. My first time in the hospital was surreal. The lights were so fluorescent, the walls were painted the color of a bursting bubblegum. It was like an advert from the twentieth century, but it was made worthwhile of Lifta's self-delivery as he jumped off of the belt and jumped towards me. I bent my legs and let my arms swiftly go under his back and knees as he jumped into my chest. I held him in my arms, standing, for a moment before the nurse coughed.

"You're going to want this," she said and handed me a navy sleeping bag.

"Why?" I asked, dumb-founded.

She smiled and answered, "He's your player, right? They all need sleeping bags. That's how you catch them. He must really love you to go to you without one."

My mother told me, "All of them are orphans, none are raised like you."

"Where do orphans come from?" I sometimes asked.

"Mommies and Daddies," she spoke-sang to me from her bed.

I once thought to ask what they had done to lose their children, but she had fallen asleep before I could ask. Adults, I had thought absently.

Besides that, the lab work, and all of the maps around town and in houses, I knew nothing about the world outside of my town. Seas to the south and actual forests, not just vacant plains and long grass in towns named Irresc like mine, were to the East.

When I came back to town, my mother understood and my uncle explained some of the things I now know to have players, raise orphans, and make money to circulate the economy for his generation while doing it. I grew to understand the orphans that adolescents raised as lucky to get a purpose from them. He has an idea about what kind of caretaker adolescents and young adults could be, but I have since learned his generation and my mother's were highly out of touch with the way things now worked. I didn't fault them for the human progress, like I didn't fault the first wave of philosophers, anthropologists, and psychologists who listened to mass hysteria as majority rule and started this system.

I took the day off from collecting glass sand on the beaches of Azule to take Lifta to the hospital. For a week I had been collecting glass sand to take to a master craftsman that could make instruments out of the glass orbs that washed up on the beaches. I liked going out at early morning, eating lunch with my players, then back to collecting.

I carried Lifta against my chest, happy to gain strength while I was young enough to use it. I had to stop and rest, tenderly setting myself down to not disturb him as he looked around. Lifta once won a battle after running up to the opponent with a blanket and pillow, reassuringly tucking the opponent into a makeshift bed on the battledome stage. He did it many times after that, sometimes he would gently ease the opponent's legs from under them and always saying, "Lift up," then began to tuck a pillow underneath their head. It was that attitude of the players that made me want to raise as many as I could.

"We really let that girl and her kid get to us," I said to him jovially when he woke up.

He wrapped an arm around my neck and his hoody fell back on his head. Every orphan I had ever seen had a hat and jacket or a hoody. I thought it was to keep warm without a sleeping bag, but after I had caught them and raised them, they kept their jackets. They rarely changed clothes, at all. Lifta's white hoody had pointed, black ears dangling from the top of it. I tussled the ruddy brown hair poking from its center as I grasped him and walked with him further. When we got to the hospital, the nurse smiled weakly at him and offered two hands to take him.

When he got off the belt, he ran to me and jumped into my arms, again. I smiled as I took him into the corner shop. Its decadent interior spoke of the wealth in player healing and tools for the adolescent. I went up to a transparent freezer and opened it to take out a noni fruit chew for Lifta. He sucked it happily as I went back to the store attendant. They took the wrapper to key in its code and took an antidote out from a top-shelf when I asked for it.

With Lifta on my shoulders and tapping my head at the routines of the townsfolk that we had seen before. I took Lifta to look at the town's Battledome and we found a picnic table to sit at. I unrolled all off the sleeping bags from my backpack.

Lifta looked at me expectantly and I whistled of the rest of the players to hear. Stye was the first to emerge from under the very table we were sitting at. She frowned and tucked her hair behind her ears. The antidote was for her and I set it on the worn wood of the table. She removed her hand from her hair and tucked the bottle into the pocket of her letterman jacket with a whisper of a nod.

Next was Grit from behind a bush, his white wild dog pelt flapping as he bounded on all fours. His hands and arms fit into the back legs of the pelt and the front legs flopped from his shoulders. He was my youngest player at four years old and was the last orphan I had found.

Ghast paced down the street from behind a telephone pole, his white, searching eyes and white frown glowed from behind the black innards of his hoody's head. His expression only seemed to relax when Lifta grabbed his leg and tumbled with him on the ground. I sighed slowly, looking at the battledome.

"You want to," Stye said, gesturing to the arena's exterior.

"Yeah, but we're not strong enough," I said, looking at the crew I had.

She frowned and tucked both sides of her hair behind her ears. She was my strongest and oldest competitor, but she was also getting too big for the hospital nurses to carry when she got hurt. I brought her antidote for the mild injuries she got. If I took her into the battle dome and she got seriously injured, we could be separated forever. I looked at her, she was fifteen now, old enough to be raising players and catching orphans.

"If you fight here, you might lose and then become an adolescent," I told her and her eyes threw themselves open. Her eyebrows disappeared behind her veiling bangs as she continued to look at me, wildly upset. I willed her to speak. A competitor has to be able to yell, to give orders, I thought. She continued to look at me, shaking her head, no.

"If you lose, there is no choice on my part," I said. I realized it sounded scary, her alone with only a sleeping bag and a starter player, like Grit, in the wild grasslands, forests, and caves.

Frightened, she pushed up from the wood of the picnic bench and sat on one of my legs. I patted her back as I positioned her legs further from my body. Ghast and Lifta looked up, mid-tousle, watching her shake with fear.

She had worn shorts and long black socks with a double band of white at the top, and a letterman jacket since I had first found her up a tree. She had fallen into the sleeping bag I was holding beneath her when Lifta, only six then, had climbed up half the tree and began lifting the branch she was on, shaking her until she fell. She was twelve and now she was fifteen. Her shorts caught on my thumb and I felt her skin under my finger. I picked her up by the waist, my fingers enclosing on her ribs like tongs to place her back on the bench next to me, but she shook at the ankles and put her shins over my thigh. Her hands folded around my neck in terror and I shook my head.

"I have to protect you," I told her. "Every way I can."

I noticed the trimmed hedges around the battle dome and watched around the picnic benches. The hedges showed the clean cut earth-orientation of the dome leaders. The town was dressed up with all of the trimmings of a well sponsored state town. Fascism is the twisting of good into evil with rabble-rousing rhetoric, barriers, suppression, hate. State government using terror reveals despotic nature. When you see it in people versus person, country versus country, player versus player, you are being shown hate, it is not just in or even in the country's leaders. What was it then that veiled the world in a happy facade while that was happening behind closed doors?

I remembered a rule the broken gov't systems had taught me. Do not create division within your own ranks. When some of the conglomerate country begins to detest itself, it's like an auto-immune disorder and it will all attack itself.

I watched Grit and Lifta play-fighting as Ghast kicked stones around the sidewalk. I turned to Stye.

She looked up at me, slowing the twisting of her hair with her fingers, "Yes?"

"Want to play a game?" She cocked her head and I put a mouthful of pocket bread to much on before I explained the instructions of red light, blue light.

She had all three orphans I had named and put together line up some twenty feet away while she called blue light when they should go and red light to stop. The first to reach her ended up laughing the hardest at her feet.

I examined each child's strength and weakness in the sprint. Lifta was the greatest as he could run fast on all fours or quickly on just his two feet, while Grit was perpetually running on all fours. I wondered how that would hurt him, but I had only been training him a year. Ghast was the worst at it, as he was simply the spectre of an A.I. that had found himself a form, albeit a flimsy black cloud and three white shapes that fit into his hoody and skinny jeans combo. No feet protruded from his tight jean's cuffs. He said he didn't like feet. Why have them if the form wasn't a necessity either? I don't know how long he had been in his body, but he was an orphan until I wrapped him up in a black sleeping bag and called him mine.

I watched them running. Stye yelled to them, occasionally turning her back and smiling at them, concerned and aware of all of them. When I became an adult, she would become the adolescent for all of them, and some I had in daycare, a secret I still kept from her. My biggest fear was being taken away to my housing regiment before I could tell her I believed in her.

Ghast came over to the bench where I was one moment pecking at my food, the next shoveling it in. I was hungrier than ever before.

"What is going on here?" He asked, pointing at the array of food.

I decided to really stop eating to say, "Adults and children like to know that when trouble comes, there is somebody that will own it and act for everybody." He nodded and I said, "Adolescents and young adults taking care of them need more sleep, food, and relaxation than them, maybe because of that responsibility."

He nodded, said, "While children are all physical, adults are all mental, and adolescents are the only ones that can hold the two together to get anything done."

I looked at him, his open white mouth seemed contrived, 8-bit, "Which are you?"

"Humans all think, 'A, B, or C?' without thinking of the fourth option." He winced his eyes so they were upside-down crescents, "Or the fifth or sixth."

"I get it. As an A.I., though, will you never get to become an adult?"

He looked at me after a pause and said, slowly, "I will never have to."

I laughed, "That's good because humans show we care for those that make us happiest by making them very, very sad."

"Oh, I've been made very," his white eyes grew even more oblong in front of his misty black head as he spoke, "very sad. But only as a spectre. Some men and women did do things I never expected to see. They, you humans would say, surprised me."

"Your knowledge extent as a human is only the basis of mass government where I'm from."

Ghast had told me odd things. Like, if I could do maths I could tell the Earth is a sphere by watching lunar eclipses. I could measure the size of Earth with a fraction of the distance because I knew that the Earth's shape is 360 degrees.

"I want to know why I'm here today," I had asked, "taking care of children by having them get in fights for money while the adults lounge around."

"Democracy and technology's applications should be in the hands of the individual," he said. "It was not. It was at once free, then their dark ages came, then the withholding ceased and it was flooded at them, adults, in a way that it sustained every one of their lives. To take care of them is," he searched for the words, "beyond their skill set."

He got off the bench to stretch in front of me and smiled wryly as he said, "Do you know," he inhaled, "that only in the first part of the twentieth century did you have a revised knowledge of a moving universe, that is not static, but expanding because of Einstein and Hubble. It then took you a century after they let you know about that to realize that our galaxy is under the same jurisdiction and that it, too, is decentralizing and expanding. It goes the same way to your own knowledge about gov't. "

"Don't say that!"

"No?" He smiled wryly again, "I am censored. The first year of the Anonymous movement in the 2010's taught me that. But you never put a good idea somebody else has researched or theorized to make a better place quickly? Do you? Do you know how many populations were killed when your former government," he really drew out the word and I shuffled my feet, speaking before he could.

"Go in your sleeping bag," I said to him and he did. He was the easiest orphan to train because he wasn't human, I thought. The nagging to visit my mother and uncle and fight out if I could even use him as a player grew like a stone in the gut. I feared the answer, but continued to smile while I played with Lifta by spinning him around until his feet came off the ground. His cherry red hair fell out of his hoody and the ears on it dangled around buoyantly.

That day outside the battle dome, I leaned into Stye, "Even if I'm not training you as hard as anyone else, that's only because you've already gotten to the highest level you can be at against these trainers. She turned and mumbled into her heavy jacket's shoulder. I smiled graciously and she ran off to the other kids that were playing. I had watched three groups enter the battle dome and saw two go to the hospital on other adolescents shoulders.

Grit came up to me, barking, and I picked him up, turned him to face the shrubbery a grass field away, and threw him. His white dog pelt flapped in the air and he rolled into a ball as he hit the branchy mess. He reappeared almost instantly from the undergrowth and came bounding back to me. I grabbed him and looked him in the eyes, the only visible part of his face behind the jaw and cheeks of the dog hood. I could hear him breathing like a dog with an open mouth and his eyes squinted in excitement.

"Where to?" He pointed, his hand loosely embedded in one of the back legs of the pelt enough for him to stick out his index finger. I grunted and threw him to the second lowest limbs of the tree he was pointing at and gasped as he was in the air, then his feet and hands were on the tree, holding him close to the trunk on a low branch.

He turned to me and I smiled, giving a thumbs-up.

But A Game

    I absolutely know I'm nearing the portion of my life when I need to buckle in my seatbelt and go for the main quest. Actually, I'm absolutely at that point in my life. What I need to do now is get to that boss, kill his or her first form, run around their crumbling castle, then kill their final form. But, instead of doing that, I keep distracting myself with side quests.

    I spent five hours walking around my girlfriend's hometown until I started running into enemies. It was then I knew I was progressing.

    Of course, it couldn't just be them, though. It couldn't just be, swing your sword, kill everyone, advance. There was a puzzle. I had to use logic to get myself to the chest, but when I did was I surprised. Of course, I held it over my head. Of course, I oggled it until the music stopped pulsing in my ears. She was thrilled. She said that she wished she could show it to her father, the king.

    We both knew she couldn't, of course. If he had still been there, or perhaps if she had been given her natural right to the throne, we wouldn't be fighting off dead bodies that pulled themselves out of the ground every night or in the market square. I wouldn't see a tool laying on the ground and immediately pick it up and begin carrying it as a weapon. If only, but alas, life was cruel.

As I partook on a side quest to gain a new heart, I got jumped by a roving band of enemies. What doesn't kill you gives you experience points, though, and I was able to not only get past them, but gained a few potions from their corpses, as well.

My girl started getting after me that night and, I guess, I started realizing that I couldn't be intimidated by the main quest, anymore.

"Look at you," she cajoled. "Look at how you've leveled up."

I looked down at the pink sheen of her dress. She never wore anything else. She was that kind of girl.

"I know," I told her.

"I am so happy that you're strong enough," she touched my arm, "to save us all."

"Oh, I'm strong enough," I said, staring into her eyes as I did. It was in that moment that I saw her tilt her head to kiss me.

Before I could turn my own head and kiss her, as well, though, she was being pulled back. As she grew further away, I saw a crystal wrapping around her midriff and heard a deep, glutinous chuckling.

It was the boss.

I took my sword and shield from behind my back and took a ready stance.

It was time.

FIRST TWO CHAPTER FROM
With Kindness

Chapter One

A weak bleat of a cow brought Lane to focus on her work. The pule did nothing but remind her of the contrived efforts at hand as she took inventory of the breakfast danishes, then the cupcakes, and later the cookies. She looked over her work, dissatisfied with an err in numbers and twirled her pencil to erase and recalculate.

Again came the petition from the cow for any human hand to take a moment out of their day and find it a better place to graze. It had found a way onto the veranda, trapped close to the bakery's back egress and, swinging its neck left and right, its call for help started off quietly, then gained to be rich in timbre, before being cut off quickly as it continued to gape in longing towards a patch of virescent grass that sat nestled

FIRST TWO CHAPTER FROM
With Kindness

between roots of a mango tree and the smoky bricks of the cloister.

Because she didn't find it a sonorous call at all, Lane did not focus on where the cow's entreaties were calling from and where it was crying out to go to as she continued her work. Moments passed, with no hint from the cow that it would cease its mooing.

"Quiet that cow, would you?" She bleated herself, this time to a passing coworker.

The individual in question did so much as fan a paper in the air near the calf's face and vociferate, "Out with you!" before speaking more demurely towards the woman entering in from the cloister, "Oh, hello Harper!"

A woman's attenuate body entered through the brightly painted pillars of the veranda's ingress.

Lane noticed promptly "Harper, I was beginning to wonder about you. "

"Hello," came the pacifying resonance of Harper's voice as she patted the calf's head and walked onward past it and into the open-air office. With a clipped tone she asked, "Is work defunct, Lane?"

Lane mirrored Harper's curt fashion, "Nearly."

Harper turned and felt for the cow's tether, then pulled herself and beast into the courtyard.

FIRST TWO CHAPTER FROM
With Kindness

Her head fell back while her eyes watched the three drones, their black triangular forms moving noiselessly across the blue sky and sighed out.

Before they were out of sight her head had dropped and she was searching the area around herself for a sufficient place to detain the cow. Without hesitation, she tied him to a cherry stained wooden pew and returned to lean against the tapered ingress, shielded from the sky by the veranda's cover. She idly began watching Lane's emaciated umber hair brush the broadsheet that she worked above before her hands momentarily ceased operating to tuck it behind her ear and tighten the elastic band's hold on the bun.

Cognizant of attention upon her, Lane made soft sighing sounds and utterances as she appended the records to the final report, indistinctly denoting an advancement in her tasks. With a low whine she closed the files and filed the paperwork.

"Now, my love," Harper declared as Lane turned from the work, "what is it we should do to quell that agitation and unease you have?"

Disconcerted at her temperance having shown, Lane's smile faded, only to return as she said, "I have a few ideas." Her eyes glittered as she swallowed her self-restraint, "Though none of them are very work-appropriate."

FIRST TWO CHAPTER FROM
With Kindness

"Darling, you're off the clock and just salacious." Harper sidled up to the window on the south side of the office. Moving her hands briskly, Lane clutched Harper's legs and pulled them over her hips. She carried the woman out of the egress and into the cloister.

Upon their arrival a pair of doves made their decampment from the innards of the mango tree known with shrill mewls and flutterings of their wings. The calf remained immersed in its own chewing and the women sat entwined on the very pew Harper had tied it to.

The reverberations from the three returning drones disunited the two as they journeyed out of the cloister, passing under many pastel or neon painted ingresses and egresses, their curved shapes betraying the restoration efforts that had been undertaken after fortifying the shaken buildings. They took themselves ever further from the district Lane worked in until they were on footpaths were cement and asphalt did not dare broach.

The duo slowed when their ears alighted with a sound much like that of an approaching biplane. Soon, though, more bees had added themselves and they began to sound more like a group of children, until they approached the hive and found themselves surrounded by the sound of the background noise of a short wave radio. Harper, being the more daring of the two, approached the beehive they paid a monthly fee to use. Her delicate hands slipped into the cadmium, thick, rubberized gloves that sat on a stand feet from the hive. She slid out one of the drawers and set it on the edge of the table, poking the propolis layers of each cubicle and then, tilting the drawer over a fresh jar from the stand, she let the blond molten food fall into the container.

When she was done, she had slid the drawer back into the hive's cubicle. With an arresting stroke of her gloved hand, she decontaminated the ostensible areas of it clean and dropped it into her shoulder-bag. Besotted with Lane, she was glad to be able to join hands with her again, after removing the bulky gloves, and they walked on.

"Any air-strikes today?" Lane asked.

"Not in Sporat," Harper nodded solemnly as she spoke, "But in Kalcache and Jesup, yes."

"Casualties?" Lane asked as she twirled her body to sit under a palm tree. She unbridled her clothing and leaned against the trunk.

"Only a dozen because of the evacuation. The crafts were from Moscow." Harper did not sit as she stood formally. This was her form of bereavement.

Off-handedly, Lane said, "They don't always seem to be from Moscow."

FIRST TWO CHAPTER FROM
With Kindness

"We tracked the one in Jesup from an ally back to them, actually."

"Why do you think they're afraid to hit mainland with their own airliners?"

Harper was about to begin to state her opinions, but the movement of the palm's leafy tendrils caught her discerning eye and as she began to objectively think of its movements, she thought to say, "I've been at the office all day; I really don't want to take it home."

Lane patted the sandy grass next to her and Harper sat. Lane removed the wedges off of her wife's feet. Harper sat in a reverie, watching Lane work at her feet. Her mind happened to filter out anything but the rumination on Lane's body as she moved about, picking up Harper's shins and setting them on her lap, then moving her hand up and down the abductor muscles of her thigh, as dark as a dried Mission fig and darker than any cursory time in the sun could ever produce on Lane's own body.

When Lane looked to her for validation, Harper jutted her chin out and kissed her jawline thrice before reaching her mouth and finding the inside quickly. They started a series of languorous kisses that de-escalated unhurriedly into inertness. For a quarter of an hour, the stasis prevailed and the two were wrapped in the arms of the other.

FIRST TWO CHAPTER FROM
With Kindness

Chapter Two

Harper was again in her wedges, stamping them against the tiles of the executive offices as she remonstrated, "Reports! Informes! Ahora, now! Why not now?"

Her forty winks were over and the phrase, "Never the twain shall meet," was competing for attention in her gray matter as she felt the longing for the indolence she had shared with Lane during a time that remained in the past hours, wholly removed from the present moment.

"Lo sentimos mucho, I'm sure," Harper said as a staffer thrust themselves into her office.

"Estoy-" said the operative.

Harper shook her head as she opened the file, "You are?"

FIRST TWO CHAPTER FROM
With Kindness

They shook their head vigorously for her, "Trieste."

"Be sorry somewhere else," she said vehemently. There was bad news in the file. Her body slumped down to hold itself up no more. Her spine pressed against the plush brown leather of the chair and she held her natural hair in her hands, knowing full well that it would mold to the shape of her palms and look uneven and dismantled after this moment.

In this moment, though, she needed to cradle her own self. Without any more irresoluteness, she grabbed for her phone from her desk, sliding it and entering her password before opening it to the background of her and Lane.

She touched the corner of the screen and pulled on the phone to lengthen it into a larger tablet. She selected an icon and waited for it to open. When it did, she was swiping her fingers along the screen and an icon of Lane's face was opening and dialing.

As she recognized her wife on the tablet's screen, Lane was saying, "Heya!"

Harper sighed into her palm, letting signs of her bereavement register on the screen for Lane to see, saying, "Hey, pet."

"I didn't expect to hear from you this early." Harper watched the screen to see that Lane's eyes sparkled as her timbre wavered, like a pubescent boy's, "Is everything okay? Should I start us a dinner or should we just go out?"

Without being redundant, Harper said, "I'm going out of the country tonight." She let her head fall into her hands again and the globular black of her hair become all that Lane could see on her screen.

"That's okay, honey. There really is no problem with that." Lane cocked her head, wishing she could reach out a hand and pick up the face she saw falling. "You do all that you can, already. You do."

Harper was looking back up now, a smirk creating highlights of white dimples on her face and, looking at her own screen, Lane didn't know if Harper's cheeks were shiny from tears or natural oils. In any event, she made soft sounds of comfort to her and upended her eyebrows in apologetic concern for her wife.

Harper looked up, away from Lane and shook her head, disturbed at who she saw. "Escapar, you!" Harper railed against the man at the door, who was there to collect the files back from her. Again, she spoke to him, "Salir," before walking over to the door and closing it, without a brief look at him.

"Will you come back tonight?" Lane asked with hesitation in her voice and a smile on her face when Harper returned to sit in front of her phone.

FIRST TWO CHAPTER FROM
With Kindness

"You can count on it," Harper nodded, feeling the need to trace the outline of Lane's jaw against the touch screen of her tablet. Her smile widened, gratified to be able to act out the impulse to feel closer to Lane.

From the main room of the building Harper heard the resounding sound of a drill. Her eyes shifted worriedly, then refocused on Lane, saying tersely, "Got to go, now. Expect me around eighteen." She watched Lane nod as she swiped the call closed on the screen. She folded the phone into a loose cylinder and shoved it in her dress' pocket.

A new man was at the door, speaking rushedly, "Do not collect your things, walk slowly, and join the group to form a single file line."

"Real talk right now, I am running and I am taking my bags," she adjusted her clothing after throwing her purse and tech bag over opposing shoulders. "Thank you for your concern that I wouldn't join the cattle, though." The man's shoulders seemed to plummet as he watched her exit her office. He moved out of the way as she withdrew keys from her pocket and shook them expectedly. "I need to lock up." She shoved them through the keyhole, the ridges of it snapping into the places it knew well before being removed and put into the recesses of Harper's purse.

FIRST TWO CHAPTER FROM
With Kindness

"Better join the herd," Harper said, jutting her jaw toward the throng of staffers exiting the building to stand, waiting for impossibilities in the cloister. Nodding, he sprinted toward them. Harper shook her head, dissatisfied with what she would have once considered inferior behavior, but today it was useful to her and for that, she was obliged to hinder her vexation.

Her fingers clasped the silver-plated handle of her Oldsmobile in the parking lot, pulling stiffly and putting her bags in before she herself entered. Its low grumbles begged for disengagement but her feet pushed against its worn peddles, unmoved as it wheezed and importuned for retirement. Pedestrians walked across the streets alongside her car, no yearning to stay to their sidewalks but rather walking freely across the cracked and weary pavement of the roads. She drove heedfully, something that led to many people's bewilderment. So often she was enacted to do things that only she was comfortable doing, like becoming a vigilante of the road, that she rarely took passengers, besides Lane.

"Hey, I know you're doing a lot right now, but I just found out the president has issued a new reform," Lane said to Harper as she arrived to their home.

Harper was an etched mask of intrigue, but concern leaked into her words as she asked,

FIRST TWO CHAPTER FROM
With Kindness

"What is it? Does it have to do with the hostile relations?"

Lane looked surprised to hear the strange alternative, "No, not at all. All electronic chargers are now mandated to be the same size and shape. No more having forty different chargers for everything." Lane had been more surprised and excited about what had seemed like an improvement, but Harper's supposition put it into the perspective of global crisis and it seemed much more meaningless, now.

A tight smile was on Harper's lips, "That's great, but it's going to take awhile for everything in Cuba to convert."

Lane was simply regurgitating the news now, "The reform is countrywide and special measures will be taken to ensure the alleviation of all citizen's qualms in the matter."

"You don't really believe what you're saying, pet?"

"Not after you contrast it with hostile relations, no."

"Good, I don't want to leave knowing you lost your marbles."

"Harper," Lane began and her wife had her eyes on her quickly. "It's not getting better, is it? I know you can't say much, but I can tell, just from watching the news."

FIRST TWO CHAPTER FROM
With Kindness

Harper sighed, pretending to be distracted and asked her, "What does the news tell you?"

"They'll bring up big crisis after big crisis and then without ever talking about the resolution to those, they'll bring up an itty-bitty thing like this and pretend that it's been solved when that isn't the problem," Lane said.

"You know what the Krussians used to do?" Harper leaned her head over to Lane's.

"What would they do?" she asked back.

"When there was something really terrible that happened within their borders, the media reported on something that had happened somewhere else, to get the citizens' minds off of the internal problems. It got to the point that when some Krussians, smart Krussians, heard reports of disasters in foreign countries, they would call their friends outside of Krussia to hear about what had happened in Krussia."

"They're land hungry. They have all of the power a country could want, but they want land, right?" Lane asked.

"It's much more complicated than that," Harper tilted her jaw away from Lane and stroked it idly.

"Hostile relations are the real problem. An impending world war is the problem."

Harper's arms were over Lane's shoulder and she began swaying her hips, "We've been in an impending World War for decades with Krussia, I don't think you are going to change that much of it by being angry about it.

Lane turned her body away and said, "You slight me with your under-estimation, Harper."

"You are so cute when you're worried."

"Don't marginalize my concerns," Lane protested as Harper's hands wrapped around her waist.

They shuffled around the floor, dancing slowly. Lane's head fell to Harper's shoulder, steadied by Harper's hand on her hair. She stroked it playfully, knowing she wouldn't have the opportunity to touch tendrils of hair like hers for days, and so, she treasured it now.

"No fresh food," Lane muttered.

"That's no good," Harper said. "Let's go to the plot?"

Lane smiled, giving a soft, "Mhmm."

Harper changed shoes and Lane grabbed a well-used bag and they trotted out the back door, past the porch, and behind their garden to a long trail with no foliage coverage. They held hands on their walk and Lane leaned against Harper again, letting her be mindful of their stride for the both of them. When they got to the large community garden plot area, they found the cherry tomatoes on the vines near the entrance were ripe and Lane ran back to a basil plant they had found to pick from it.

"Mint water tonight," Harper called to Lane. Obedient, Lane bounded toward the mint that covered a table-sized patch of ground and bundled some up. They walked back and cooked a dinner together before Harper received a message and got into a black SUV, destined for the airport. Lane waved and stood in their home's entrance for moments, counting the feelings she had pass through her before feeling contented to be alone. Only then did she return inside.